Tren

David Meah

Published November 2016
Published by David Meah

First Printing: 2016

ISBN Enter your 978-1-326-81672-8

CONTENTS

Acknowledgements

I would like to thank my family without whose help this book would never have been completed.
Thank you for your patience and guidance

Thank you Daryn Reeds for your assistance. The contribution of your time and effort in the letters in chapter three.
Your help in bringing this book to life.

Andy Hall for all the phone calls bugging you for your opinion and guidance.

Most of all to all the readers who have taken the time to acknowledge and read my work. Thank you.

David

INTRODUCTION

In a time of chaos and disorder. The European nations now warring against each other, gaining nothing more than an extreme loss of human life.

Germany are placed as the antagonist spreading their forces though out Europe, eradicating anything in their path, the United Kingdom and their allies as the guardians struggling to preserve the right of freedom. It's hard to believe that the death of one man could spiral into one of the bloodiest wars known to man.

The assassination of the Archduke Franz Ferdinand of Austria, on the 28th June 1914.
The fuel that fired the First World War.

This was a time of great unrest, the world of many torn apart, a time of doubt and sadness, a time sworn that would never be repeated again...

Chapter 1: Moving in

Deep in the war torn country of France. April 1917.

The dark clouds hiding the skies over the landscape, the sounds of gun fire and explosions echo in the darkness of night. The spiraling smoke from the barraged towns and villages in the distance cloaking the moon from sight. The rain finally subsiding after two hours of downpour.

The walk is hard and the ground is uneven underfoot, the bog like surface snatching at their feet with every move. The eight men are wet, miserable and fatigued, yet alert, scanning their surroundings, mindful that the enemy could be closing in. Along the horizon flickering lights and explosions from the continuing battles taking place in the far distance can be seen and heard.

Time seems endless; trekking over the muddy marshy land. The rifle section from the 1st battalion of the rifle brigade now separated from their unit, like many others, lost in a wilderness of hate and torment. The battle worn riflemen searching for a safe haven to rest their heads.

The cold east winds tormenting, gust across them, unable to escape the chill. Sergeant Taff Taylor is leading his men. His head lowered as he struggles on, his strong tall frame, stretching the wet cloth of his tunic with his big shoulders, wrestling the wild wind and boggy terrain, his large hands cradled his Enfield rifle, the bitter cold piercing at his fingers.

Taylor came into this war from the beginning, at the age of 24, now three years on and gaining three promotions for his acts of bravery. The last time was his sergeant stripes, for retrieving his commanding officer from nomans land, during a retreat from the battles of the Ancre in November 1916.

Their Colonel of the Brigade wanted to lead the men out one last time. A man who had a family history of heroes through the decades of British military campaigns dating as far back as Waterloo.
This was to be his last battle before returning home. He wanted a story to tell his grandchildren, and a story he got to tell. He wanted his name to be echoed in history along with his ancestors.

Bullets caught him in his left leg, he fell hitting the dirt heavily. The surviving soldiers of the brigade scampering out of nomans land, heading for safety, wanting to be clear of the stray bullets from the deadly German machine gunners.

He was hit on the retreat, two bullets rip through his left leg, one exiting, ripping his calf muscle the other exploding his kneecap. Finding himself stranded in nomans land just one mile from friendly forces. Alone unable to move, the pain searing through to almost blackout point. Aware he could see his last days in this ungodly wasteland, covered in death and misery.

The survivors of the brigade had scurried back to their lines with their tail between their legs after heavy losses. Taylor watched the returning soldiers as they threw themselves into the safety of the trench, the sight of fear showing in their eyes, their tear stained faces as they hauled the wounded out of nomans land, counting the losses as the last man entered.
Corporal Taylor noticed the Colonel hadn't returned, so he set off to scour the battle torn landscape. As time passed he accidently found him.

Colonel Shackleton was sipping from his silver hip flask when Taylor accidently fell into the mud drenched crater. "Would you like a sip old man?" rasped the Colonel offering the flask, sat in a wash of murky dark clay coloured water up to his waist. "Don't mind if I do sir …But then I had better get you back to the lines, nights closing in and it's turning cold" Taylor replied a broad grin stretching across his face. Taylor was pleased he had found him and that he was still alive.

Even with the loss of his lower left leg, Colonel Shackleton wanted to show his appreciation. Colonel Shackleton had Corporal Taylor promoted to sergeant and awarded him the Military medal for bravery

Sergeant Taylor now unable to shake off the hero status found himself in command of many battles and even now with seven men behind him, all relying on him to get them home. Commanding a unit had its cost, the loss of life becoming a burden he no longer wanted or desired.

Corporal scouse Ryan followed closely, stooping as he walked.
A small slim built man, a lot stronger than he looked, a young 22-year-old of Irish descent. Ryan earned his rank through good leadership and bravery. Being an intelligent man who can think quick and get out of scrapes. Ryan never faltered, he is a reliable sort.
He joined Taylors unit with Corporal Yorkie Danns, a tall heavy built man, an old weathered faced 23-year-old, whom had worked alongside his father in the coal mines before being conscripted into this war in the early part of 1915.

Although both equal in rank they rarely saw eye to eye. Still bickering at each other as they ploughed through the marshy landscape step by step. Ryan steps into a mud filled hole, his leg getting stuck, been sucked further into the mire as he struggles unable to free himself.

Danns witnessing this, slowly swaggers over to help, grinning all the way. Ryan's pride gets the better of him pushing Danns away, now his foot sinks further and becomes immovable, almost knelt down, he finally accepts Danns offer after three minutes of getting nowhere and frustration setting in. Danns yanks Ryan's leg as Ryan struggles to free it. After a few more minutes he retains his freedom from the bog, shaking his leg like a soaked through dog.
Not a thankyou or thanks of any kind, he just adjusts his clothing and continues with his march, Danns shakes his head in dismay, shoulders his rifle and follows.

The rifleman men that followed were Harold: a skinny slight fellow mid 20's, very quiet lad who just obeys whatever command is given, he finds it hard to make friends, unable to fit in, never knowing why he volunteered in the first place.

Rifleman Clarence: a tall mean looking man, a street fighter by trade. Orphaned at a young age finding himself working in the workhouses after his family died of tuberculosis. He learnt how to fight and take care of himself, living in the streets of Manchester. At thirty years old and surviving the streets and with nothing else on offer he joined the army, only to find himself in a foreign land, fighting a war he didn't ask for.

Rifleman Conor Neville: an average height, strongly built young man in his late 20's, lives with his mother and brother on their farm.
He had taken charge after his father passed away but found himself conscripted along his brother rifleman Andy Neville: an average height, strongly built lad in his early 20's, the younger brother, who tends to rely on Conor, never leaving his side. They all joined Taylor a year ago as his reinforcements.

On tail end Charlie was rifleman Davies, an average built average height young man in his late 20's. Well educated, university graduate, a disappointment to his military family, his long line of high ranking officer kin as far back as he can remember.

Unforeseen circumstances led him to Taylor's section back in July 1916. He keeps close to the Conors, rifle in his hands, treading carefully. Looking back now and then.

The wind now cursing with the crosswinds making the march harsher, they continue their journey. Still the ground beneath snatching at their every move.

Sergeant Taylor feels a change in the air, the smell of body odour and cordite, a built up mud mound in front of them obscures something from view. "Halt!" his hand held up to exaggerate the order. The men stop instantly looking at each other puzzled. Taylor moves forward slowly; he stands isolated for a few seconds before he beckons the rest over to him.

They look down into a trench, the feeling of dread pounds their every pour, broken bodies lying in thick mud, the broken furniture and ammo boxes scattered, the dead soldier's rifles still laying perched on the edge of the trench line as if ready to engage the enemy.

Sergeant Taylor recognises the trench from battles gone by. This should be housing two full infantry regiments, welcoming them into a safe haven out of nomans land and into the security of friendly allies. This is not the welcome they had anticipated! All that was left was death and its stench.

Having nowhere else to go sergeant Taylor gives his order. "Let's get in there".

The eight-man section scramble over the side into the trench, hitting the soft muddy wet ground, the claylike mud sticking to their boots. Movement is hard with the heavy clay covered boots.

The overpowering stench forces Rifleman Andy Neville to keel over. Vomit spewing out as he coughs wrenching from the back of his throat. The mix of cordite, rotting flesh, stale piss and dampness bring him to his knees, eyes watering, he clutches his stomach.

Rifleman Conor Neville seeing his brother suffering tries to encourage him, "come on lad … you've been in worse shite than this", his West country accent adding to the hilarity. The Neville's look at each other and erupt into laughter. Conor places his hands on Andy's shoulder lapel and drags him to his feet. He places his arm around him, they smile at each other then head toward the others.

Sgt Taylor takes in the scene, the grey clay walls, the sticky muck underfoot and the hundreds of foul smelling decaying corpse laying or slumped in the mire. Not ideal, but he knows they need to stay and recoup their strength He barks out his orders. His Welsh voice strong and clear "Shift some of that shite out of the way …. this is home! Ok Corporal get the lads to clear a place. We need to get comfortable if we're here for a few days".

The men don't look heartened by the task ahead, as they turn their heads looking around at the squalor they had landed in. Taylor continues "Look for any food, ammo and anything to clear us out of this mud." He points at Ryan who now has to delegate.

Corporal Ryan immediately turns to the men, resting on his rifle repeating the sergeant's orders. "OK guys! you heard the man, let's get it sorted". With a few grunts from the team they all start moving the dead and debris from their immediate location.

Corporal Danns and Rifleman Clarence seize a body out of the mud, the sound of the sludge smacking as they remove it from the floor can be heard across the trench, the Neville's turn to look with repulsion shaking their heads.

A silver cigarette box falls from the side pocket out of the dead man's tunic, hitting the ground. Corporal Danns drops the body instantly out of his arms, he bends down and gathers the cigarette box, he wipes it on his tunic before placing it in his pocket; smiling he gathers up the deadman's body again, Clarence just looks on. The two men start to walk to the far right of the trench. Collectively the section stacks up the bodies. On clearing a large space, the section regroups.

Corporal Danns takes charge. "Neville's I want you two to grab anything that will raise us out of this shite! By the way no smoking till early light, don't want the Hun spotting us, don't forget could be those sniper bastards out there".

The two Neville's start their search; picking up large pieces of wood and corrugated tin, travelling back and forth until they have accomplished their task. During the same time Ryan and Davies search and collect canned food by the box full.

The men sit there, with spoons they scoop out the cold offerings from the crudely opened tins.
With the night fading and the men weary, Sgt Taylor stands, he approaches Danns. "Right lad…. time to get your heads down! Rota the watch Danns …any movement, I want to know straight away … no delays.

Cpl Danns absorbing the command turns his attention to the section, helmet in one hand and scratching his lice ridden head with the other; flicking his fingers as they get caught in his finger nails.
"Sure thing Taffy… will do! Davies… Harold's; you two for the first two hours then the Neville's!" he glances at his wrist watch "The time now is 02:00 hours, make sure

we're all up at first light". The men take up their sleeping positions as Rifleman Davies and Harold's collect their rifles, both taking up their positions looking out to the seemingly endless wasteland before them. The distant skies illuminated from the constant barrage of battle fire.

Chapter 2: Nomans land

06:00 hours the following day.
A clear day with warm temperatures, mist rising from the damp ground, the stench rising as the odours seep from the walls and the trench floor, the muddy sludge solidifying, cracks appearing as the heat from the sun bakes the ground. The sky is a deep blue with minimum clouds, the sound and smoke along the horizon evident the battles continue to scar the land, the trench is silent as if in another dimension.

Conor Neville kneels down to where Sergeant Taylor is sleeping. He looks at Taylor and smiles, it's the first time in long while he has seen him at peace, he takes a Sharpe intake of breath before he awakens the Sergeant.

He gently rocks the Sergeant, who slowly opens his eyes, lifting his body from his makeshift bed stretching out his arms while yawning. "Hey Sarge six o'clock" says Conor still shoving the sergeant's arm. "Cheers lad ...got a cig?" Taylor holding out his hand. Conor lights up two cigarettes and hands one over. The Sergeant smiles taking a large draw from the cigarette, releasing a plume of smoke.

Conor now back on his feet, reports the night's activity "No let up on the battle out there. Been at it all night" Sgt Taylor nods "OK lad…. let's get some grub …. are the rest up?" he hauls himself up dusting off his uniform whilst stretching.

"Yeah all up … Davies is brewing up and Danns is on watch" replies Conor. Taylor and Conor join the others. The soldiers are sitting there drinking hot tea and eating from tin cans with their spoons, content to have food in their bellies and no enemy fire raining down on them, a chance to relax and may they dare to think of home.

Danns is stood in the far right corner is looking out into the waste land sipping at his tea, keeping a vigil eye on the waste ground laid out before him. Stacked to the right of him is the wall of rotting dead flesh, he seems immune to the smell and defacement of the fallen comrades. Three overly large brown rats scurry taking their pickings from them.

Danns empties the dregs by tossing the remainder over the bodies, disturbing the rats, they scurry out over the top of the trench, he pays no mind. He returns his attention back to the wall of the dead and starts to pillage the pockets of the fallen soldiers placing the goods small enough to fit, into his pockets. The rest look on.

Davies looks on in disgust, appalled he turns to the sergeant and ask, "Does he not care; how can you rob a dead man?" Sgt Taylor smiles, shakes his head at Davies, he had seen much worse over the years, made to ignore it, men using weaker men as a tool to release sexual tension, the execution of deserters and pow's. He himself had never partaken, he found it nauseating, but was made to swear he had never seen it or spoke about it. "What's wrong with that? He's just taking it cos they don't have any use for it now."

Danns continues to probe into the pockets. Making his way down the wall, on this occasion he pulls out an envelope. He takes one looks at it, shakes his head and discards it to the muddy ground. The envelope glides towards the ground, landing half in a dark muddy puddle sinking slowly. Davies scrambles to his feet and walks over to the discarded letter, he picks it up, wipes off the mud and places the letter in his top pocket. His eyes transfixed on Danns.

Danns shrugs his shoulders pointing at Davies "What you gonna do with that … you knew this man or somat?" he says shaking his head, Davies clearly not daunted replies "No but it may have some bearing on what happened here or the name of the person who needs to know what happened to him." Cpl Dann's smirks, his deep icy blue eyes burning into the face of Davies, thinking what do you care? Just throw it away. "What of it? Chances are we're all gonna die in this shit hole any way". Says Danns looking Davies directly in the eyes. "So why take their valuables?". Davies replies, displaying discontentment looking straight back at Danns. Disgusted at the sight of him.

Cpl Danns face reddens, feelings of irritation taking hold, why should he be grilled over a dead man's belongings and what has it got to do with him, hatred seeping through grabbing at his inner core, "Get lost" he says becoming defensive. "Look no one asked for this! If I get out of here, I want to have something to show for my troubles… may be able to afford my own gaff... have something more than my old dad did... working till all hours… and for what?! A shite pays from nearly killing yourself down a bloody stinky hell hole of a coal pit… no I ain't doing that… not after this crap! I think I'm owed more than that". His head shaking and spittle releasing from his words.

Davies takes a step back, keeping a cool head shrugging his shoulders "OK pal keep your blooming hair on ...I get it ...it's just…. that's someone else's and from a dead person ...just don't seem right that's all!"
Cpl Danns now with frustration showing even more, viciously gets into Davies's face, his voice a menacing

evil tone. "Not like there gonna use it …. well is it!? Now get out of my face before I forget you're not the Hun and gift you a bullet." Davies ignores Danns threat and walks back and takes his place with others.

The hours passed, boredom setting in as the section sat in silence. Cpl Ryan and Sgt Taylor decided to go scouting the trench, to see how far it stretched and to see if anyone was still alive.

The dead bodies line the path as they walk further, deeper into the trench of death. Sgt Taylor and Ryan are baffled by the loss of life. "Wonder what happened here! Not much mess… could have been a gas attack? ... No one looks like they tried for their mask... Wonder what did all this?" asks Ryan Looking extremely puzzled as the two continue to walk on. "Look... no one survived out of all these?!" says Taylor shaking his head, Ryan nods in agreement.

The corpses lying there, no bullet wounds to be seen no damage to the uniforms, but whatever it was, it was painful! Evident in the tortured look on the faces and the twisted shape of the bodies as they lay there. As the two continue, they stumble upon a gnarled body in an officer's uniform, Ryan's mumbles as the shock starts to take its grip on him. "Must have been a painful death!" They start to go through his pockets and search for papers or any documents.

There's nothing but letters for his dearest wife, sergeant Taylor shows Ryan, "Fuck Sarge! What a waste …Who's gonna tell his missus?" Ryan's looks down at the tormented body scratching his head. Taylor doesn't reply he just replaces the letters, lowers his head and says a silent pray. The two men have seen enough and turn around and head back to the others.

Cpl Danns is the first to speak "What did you find Taffy…... how far does it stretch?" Sgt Taylor takes a drag from the newly lit cigarette, exhales the smoke whilst speaking "too far… all dead, don't make sense… no bullet wounds, no bombing! Can only think it must have been quick whatever it was ... gas attack of some kind." Still shaking his head. Cpl Ryan reaffirms the sergeant's words "I think ...like the Sarge says... no sign of mortar or artillery fire, Gotta been a gas attack or somat?"

Danns looks outward to the distance skies. The flashes still breaking up the horizon skies; large plumes of smoke blocking out the light of day. "Still going on up yonder ...not a lull at all!" he says pointing out to the sky line.

Rifleman Harold's now on watch thinks he sees something moving in the distance, he takes a second look squinting, as if that would make him see clearer. Harold's rotates quickly on the spot to face the sergeant. "Sarge … over there …think I saw something!" He points out into nomans land. The sergeant and the two corporals move with haste. Taylor removes his binoculars from the case and scans the land.

Taylor focuses the binoculars; in the far distance he sees something or someone stirring slowly; low to the ground. Sgt Taylor's arm reaches out to Danns, pulling him closer, indicating what he has seen. "Danns... you and Neville C get out there! Check this out! Bring back any docs you find… the rest of you; covering fire!" he says whilst waving his right index finger at the trench side. The section race to the trench wall, placing their rifles over the edge looking down their sights waiting for the command to fire, their bodies in alert, their adrenalin taking over.

Danns and Connor scramble over the side keeping low to the ground, the bombardment of the near towns and villages continue, their movement is slow but deliberate, the soft mud inviting them in. With every crawl movement they sink further; their uniform absorbing the wetness of the mud.

With obstacles hindering their route, the dark deep mud holes inviting them in, waiting to swallow them whole. The foul rotten smell from the decaying animals and human corpses eaten by the large brown rats, wild cats and birds causing them to heave, vomiting as it overwhelms them. The sights you would normally miss when attacking or retreating from the enemy. Danns looks back at Conor: "You see anything yet?". Conor struggling to manoeuvre in the heavy mud; breathing heavily; replies "No … can't see anything …. moving that is, apart from all that vermin".

The two men continue to struggle through the mire, arms and legs aching from the arduous task, on looking back to the trench, the two have travelled well out of normal sight. no sign of their comrades left behind. Conor clearly not happy with the situation, feeling vulnerable and trapped in the vast open space. Beads of sweat running down from his forehead, feeling even more nauseous and afraid "I don't feel good about this Danns! The guys are out of range now, Danns also feeling vulnerable; turns his head "Let's just get this done and get back… need to know what's out there!"

They continue, weaving around the shell craters formed in the ground from the artillery bombardments, avoiding the deep brown murky water holes ... they stop! something's out there.

Danns points to the large crater a yard or so away from him, his excitement showing as he rushes his words "There… just there ...in that crater! Can you see? Conor... hey can you see?"

Danns turns around, Conor seems to have disappeared. Panic seeps in, he starts looking around more frantically. The beat of his heart accelerating almost ready to explode. "Conor ...CONOR ...Conor where the fuck are you?"

A sound to the right of him coming from the mud draws his attention. Air bubbles hit the surface. "Help ...Help He…." the voice has gone.

Danns franticly scrambles over to the sound of the voice. He finds a dark mud patch; somethings moving in it. Without a second thought he plunges his right arm deep into the mud... then the other. Reaching as far down as possible; his face against the thick dark watery sludge, no time to think about the stale smell of the rancid liquid mud ...with a heavy sigh he heaves up his torso using all he has to give. The sheer weight of Conor covered head to foot in the clay like substance is no mean feat, every ounce of Danns strength is taken, his huge muscular arms aching, the pain racing through his shoulders down to his fingertips trying to gain a solid grip on Conor's tunic.

Conor hits the solid ground sending ripples through the mud. Danns breathes a sigh of relief, Conor; now frantic, fighting for breath ...clawing the mud from his face and coughing out foul dirty sludge from his throat. Danns turns his head and says "Thought I'd lost you then! What the hell?! You ok?" Conor continues spitting out and wiping away the thick mud, still fighting to breath "I think I will be". The two men lay there motionless on their backs in silence, recovering their breath.

Back at the trench, Taylor is still viewing through the binoculars. "I can't see them ...for god sake let them be alright" He looks heavenward searching for something, someone, anything to relieve the burden from his shoulders, he never asked to be the section commander, this was placed on him through his many battles, a sickening feeling fills his body, colour draining from his face.

Ryan can see Taylors anxiety in his speech and body language, he places his left hand on Taylor's right shoulder as to offer him comfort. "It'll be ok Sarge ...you'll see, Danns and Neville are old hands at this now... they know what they're doing".

Taylor's head turns as he snaps "We all know what we're doing! Just some of us shouldn't be here... we've rode our luck to near extinction. I sure believe we're out of time with it!" frustration showing. Taylor steps back from Harold's and Ryan knowing snapping at them won't make things better, he knows they all just want to get away from this war torn mess and be back in the warmth of their own homes.

In no man's land, the two scouts finally reach their target. A young boy lays there face up, half sunk in the mire: his laboured breaths, eyes dull and sunken, the tear stained cheeks show he has been there for some time. His body showing poor diet and malnutrition, his cloths worse for wear with the number of patches sewn on to his jacket evident. Possibly an orphan of the war.

Danns cradles the boy in his arms and looks him up and down. The hole ripped through his shoulder tells him what he needs to know. This poor kid must have been fleeing from imminent danger, sniper shot had got this kid, the tell-tale sign of a marksman, the shot was too clean.

Conor sickened, looks on as the child's last breath is drawn, tears start to form. "Why kill a kid?" he asks. Danns places the blood soaked kid down gently. Brushing his fingers over the child's face to close his eyes. "The Prussians don't care much for anyone but their own kind… Would have used him as range practice… I think we should head back! Conor follow my tracks …. may be safer, don't want to pull you out of any more bogs." Conor thankful to be alive; smiles. "Sure thing Danns and thanks back there... thought it was my time". Danns pats him hard on the back. "Not today son!". Danns leads on as Conor follows.

Sgt Taylors gives a great sigh of relief as the two scouts return, falling over the side into the trench "Good to see you two back… had me worried! Anything to report?"

Danns picks himself up and trying to dust down the mud covered uniform. "Found a dying kid… about 12 years I would think... Poor bastard, sniper had him ...had no chance. Be glad when we get out of here". He says shaking his head and pointing out into nomans land.

Taylor mentally inspects Conor up and down, not daring to ask what had happened or where his rifle was. "OK you two, best clean up and get a hot brew inside you."

The two soldiers acknowledge and retreat to clean themselves down.

The afternoon sun moves to the west. The stale smell of death lingers. Taylor's thoughts go out to the families of the lost.

He strides over to Ryan picking up an empty ammo box on the way "Ryan you and two others collect the dog tags, only decent thing we can do for these poor sods" Taylor extends his arms passing the wooden ammo box over to Cpl Ryan who beckons Clarence and Harrold's to join him. Without any response the trio start walking into the depths of the trench, removing the identity tags as they go.

Young Neville and Davies head for the human wall to the right and begin to retrieve their fallen comrade's tags. Sgt Taylor nods in approval, discharging a spiraling plume of smoke from his cigarette.

Chapter 3: The letters

Late evening, the sun has retreated and the half-moon spills out its light to a still quiet night, the million stars illuminated against the dark purple sky. The war has momentarily stopped. Not a sound of artillery or mortar fire, no flashes in the skies horizon, just smoke and mist dancing over the tormented landscape.

Davies sits in the foulest corner of the stinking void, gulps back some water and looks at the letter. The dirty brown envelope has one word wrote on it, Lucy. He slowly deliberately removes the pages, placing the envelope back into his trouser pocket, he shakes out a cigarette from the packet and places it between his lips, he flips his Wonderlite cigarette lighter, within an instant the flame is licking around the tip of the cigarette. He draws hard till the end is flickering and smoke is gently flowing up towards the night sky.

The page is still damp and some of the writing has run, but is still legible. He turns his gaze to the rest of the men in their makeshift beds, exhaustion catching up with them, He draw some relief at the sight of them sleeping peacefully, not fidgeting unrested as the previous nights, not able to feel safe.

His gaze reaches further down the trench… Clarence's perched at edge with his rifle ready for action anticipating enemy engagement, but not this evening, this evening is quiet, no movement, no conflict, no sound. Davies turns his attention back to the letter; he begins to read.

My dearest Lucy,

I cannot begin to tell you of my frustration at being away from you and our darling little Robert. I would exchange the world to be woken by his gentle cry and to watch you sleep on as I take him in my arms from his crib. I try not to count the days when they say we might have leave, but it is a hard thing when I so long to be with you both. I cannot say where or when we are, or the censor's scissors will be at my letter but I can tell you that we are gloriously advancing and all the fellows are in very good spirits. Rations are well stocked though a little bland and some of Mrs. Pearce's jam would stave off the monotony but please don't tell her as I fear she may become insufferable! My darling, I cannot wait to hold you both and to feel you in my arms.

Lovingly,

Stanley x

Davies raises his head, glances at the flesh decaying wall, he looks harder wondering which of the fallen this letter belongs to, a little envy creeps into his heart, to have a wife and son to go home to, how beautiful that would be. Davies raises his head towards the night sky, with his eyes closed he digs into his deepest thoughts. Transporting himself to another place and time. He's sat on his comfy regal armchair next to his wood burning fire place, the flames of yellow and blue dancing upward, flickering sparks floating up high in the chimney, his Lucy knelt on the deep pile rug leaning on his knee, her head in her hands gazing at him with her beautiful green eyes, Robert sleeping in his crib at the side of Davies's chair.

A smile appears from the corner of his mouth. Without a moment's notice tears cascade down his cheeks, who's he kidding there's no wife or child waiting for him. Home is a million miles away or so it seems, he knows he's a whole world away and may not even survive this war, the image disappears. He lowers his head and commences to read the second letter.

My Darling,

We're moving up Lucy, and I have to say we are full of hope and optimism that this is a decisive push. The generals seem certain that when we break this line, the Axis will crumble and we will drive on at an alarming pace. I received post from Tom at the store so please thank him for that and it truly cheered me to learn of things at home.

To hear that Robert now sits unaided makes me realise all that I have missed and I long to be home again with you both. I long to hold my son but more my darling I long to hold you and kiss you. There is nothing else that would keep me from you except that I must do my duty. With God's strength and I will be home soon. My love to you both,
lovingly
Stanley x

A sudden sadness take hold of him, he feels the lump in his throat, his mouth dry, he sinks his head into his hands; sobbing, knowing this woman, this child will never see this brave soldier again. A few minutes later he regains his composer and neatly folds the paper and returns it to its envelope and places it back in his pocket.

Davies tilts his head skyward. pleading words to the heavens, "If you can hear me Lord … please let this war be over" quivering in his tone, silent tears stream from his dark swollen eyes "Please let's stop this now... if you are there… you must know… I know you know… it's taken too many lives. Please God…. stop this now." He breathes a heavy sigh and slumps against the trench wall.

He places another cigarette between his lips, lights it then raises to his feet, takes a few steps forward and adopts the sentry position, his eyes looking down the rifles line of fire.

Chapter 4: A river runs through

Night slowly turns into day, the low clouds hanging over dark skies, it's going to be a wet day. The wind picks up, the men feel the cold coming in. Rain starts gentle, picking up pace mixed with a cocktail of harsh winds, now the rain is a torrent downpour; soaking everything it meets. The eight-man section are huddled up under the makeshift ridged tin shelter, water seeping in from the gaps between the tin. The rhythmic tune as it bounces off the shelter becoming frustrating.

Their uniforms dark and heavy from the rain, there's no escaping the damp. The cold biting hard on the flesh as the cold dampness seeps through to the core combined with the chill from the bitter winds.

Danns now soaked through and cold, fidgeting unable to get comfortable starts his gripe. "Well if this keeps up it won't be a bullet that gets you …bloody hyperthermia will! Look at us huddled up like vermin, soaked through like trench rats". He raises his voice, he wants to be heard, the men just looking down, arms clutching around their knees trying to keep dry. "No one cares much if we live or die, we're just numbers… 'get over the top… your country will remember you…' bastard generals." He says

Spitting into the puddles forming water rings around their feet.

Sgt Taylor sits up straight and attempts to play it down "Well no need to worry about the Hun…. dare say they will be all tucked up nice and warm". Cpl Ryan replies in bitterness "Yeah just like the Ponzi generals, sat on their fat arses; drinking tea. Do you think if we get back we'll be treated as heroes?" his head shaking from side to side as he speaks.

Sgt Taylor's face looks deep in thought. He looks at the sodden men, the wanting of home showing through. "Would like to think so after three and half years. The things we've seen and done, I wouldn't wish this on anyone" he says wiping the rain water from his face. Taylor continues to talk, the men huddle up transfixed like school children, sorrow showing on in his face, he looks distant as if in another time and place.
"This war has almost broken me … I find it hard to believe men can do this to each other. Politics, 'king and country' they count for nothing out here. I remember my first day, all keen and raring to go…., couldn't wait for my first kill." He shakes his head. "killed too many men now! Too much blood and guts on my hands. I hope this ends soon, It's got to be the last war this world will ever see." The men nod in agreement.

Clarence; shaking with cold starts to stutter "Sarge ...do you not think we would be better off going further down the trench? I saw a couple of pockets were these men had dug out sleeping quarters! Would be better than sitting here drowning in this shite."

The water level rises rapidly as the rain continues to hammer down, ripples made with every drop into the newly formed river on the trench bed.

The men now stood ankle deep in dark murky water. Sergeant Taylor responds to Clarence. "Yes ...sure thing Clarence. Lead the way… anything has to be better than this." The rain saturating them from their helmets to their boots.
The section grabs their belongings, Conor Neville with his newly acquire rifle from one of the fallen. They follow Clarence in a westerly direction deeper into the trail of dead soldiers, trying to be sure footed as the fallen bodies sink further under them, deep into the mire that had been created.

Some ten minutes later and a lot of negotiating, keeping a steady footing to get there, they enter a large dugout cut into the side of the trench. Carved neatly making a good sized living quarter, shuttered with wooden sleepers holding the ridged tin in place, a warm dry haven from the battering raging winds and rain. These must have been used for the officers of the company. There was evidence of their stay as maps still lay exposed on the table, demonstrating the battle formations and prelims on what was meant to happen.

The dust covered unopened bottle of dark rum is a welcome sight. It's the first thing Ryan does. He removes the cap from the bottle and takes 3 long swigs, the heat from the alcohol warming him inside as it flows. He passes the bottle to Taylor who repeats this as did all the others till the bottle had returned to Ryan, who finished the last few drops before tossing the bottle out of the dugout. No one spoke, they just searched the room for dry clothing. On finding what they needed, they stripped out of their wet clothes and changed. It was still raining heavy and bitterly cold outside.

The sleeping quarters were silent, they fall asleep, fatigue taking over. No one was on sentry duty this night. Taylor knew that no army would send men into battle in these conditions, they were more likely to lose men from the elements than the cost of a bullet.

Chapter 5: Moving out

The weather had calmed down; the sun was high breaking through the clouds. The river had started to disappear, soaked up by the sun beating down on the bed and trench walls, leaving a thick dark muddy sludge. The overpowering smell of rotten flesh and dampness as the steam raises, leaving an eerie mist covering the dead.

Danns is the first to stir. He removes his damp boots, revealing sockless feet, the deep cracks, red sores, dirt stained broken toenails blackened from old cuts.
He reaches out to the dry rag hanging over the back of the chair and rubs his feet dry vigorously. Reaching inside his satchel he produces a beaten tin of powder, he begins to shake the tin covering his feet, whilst massaging his heels and in between his toes.
The aching in his feet relieved, a dry foot is so pleasing for him, using his army knife he cuts away at the hard built up skin on his heel. He continues to powder them vigorously, smiling broadly content with the feeling of warm dry feet.

During his search for the dry clothing, he found some decent dry boots in good condition, housing socks. He places these on his feet, continually smiling his face shows how much this means to him. Warm dry boots with socks, something he had not had for the last four weeks.

Within the next hour the men were awake and tucking into a variety of canned foods. Each man passing it around as to share the bounty they had come across the previous evening. A large metal chest at the rear of the room, housing quality canned food, consisting of fruit to fish and vegetables. They relished the banquet, mopping up the last dregs with the foiled wrapped oat biscuits.

Sgt Taylor picks up his rifle, disgusted by what he sees, dirt covering the barrel and sight, he orders the section, "Check your weapons!... Give them a good clean... Never know what can happen?"

The section carries out their duty without fuss, getting on with the cleaning of their Enfield rifles, showing how disciplined they have become. On completion the Sargent checks all the rifles individually, at the same time checking how many rounds they have per man. The section is well stocked, each having eight full magazines in both pouches.

Outside the familiar sound of battle can be heard in the distance.

"I See they back at it." says Harold's his face lacking the enthusiasm to carry on as he skulks further back into the dugout.

Andy Neville moves towards the entrance, popping his head out for a glance he looks out of the dugout. "Sounds like it's getting closer; ... Could be just a few days and they will be here." Taylor follows young Neville out of the dugout.

"You could be right there Neville... We need to start making our way to the beach, if we are ever to leave this forsaken land... Will take a good week if we set off now; Ryan, Danns search for rations: Fresh water... and some grenades wouldn't go amiss." Pointing at the two men.

Davies questions with a puzzled look "Who are they fighting Sarge? ... We were beaten at Marne some weeks ago now... They can be only the odd drifting section like us, dispersed; Trying to get to friendly lines or home"

Sgt Taylor explains "The French have a strong hold near here... must be them... Don't sound like they can hold on much longer?... The Germans have pushed on with momentum these last few weeks... I just hope the rumours are true". "What rumours are they?" asked Neville shrugging his shoulders. "The allies have capitalised in Paris, if that falls" Taylor takes in the faces looking straight at him... "It's over for us all... it won't take them long to drive us all in the sea and I do mean drive us in" He knew if the Germans ever got to this point they would be no mercy for the allies, destroying them before they could make it back home. Continued Taylor looking at Neville, who nods in acknowledgment.

Danns and Ryan split the section and carry out their details, collecting the supplies they need from various locations of the trench. Sgt Taylor studies the open map laid out on the table.

The men regroup on their return, Taylor shows them the position there at and where he wants to get to. Taylor starts his brief. "Right... now we have all regrouped... Let's get started... Need to make our way to that tree line. Keep formation... no stragglers... need to get there fast, I don't know what's out there". The section knows what could be out there, they know it only takes a second or so to be caught out.

With their adrenalin reaching boiling point the soldiers make their way over the edge, they can see the tree line. There's just over 200 meters of the discarded battle worn land to cross. Laden with broken carts, dead horses, soldiers and then the barbed wire, twisting in all directions. The craters from the heavy shelling that had taken place many days before in-between, acting as obstacles in their route. After clearing all that there's about 1,500 meters of open grassland to cross to reach the woodlands

The men reach the top, standing with their backs to the trench. A sudden tremor erupts from the trench, the ground beneath them shaking.

They turn in unison to witness the hoard of brown rats. Tens of thousands immerse over the rotten corpse of the fallen soldiers, feeding on the eyes. Tugging relentlessly, burrowing through the flesh, reaching the stomach organs. Ripping away at the intestine, liver and rotting kidneys. Even the battle harden Taylor finds this too much. The eight-man section keeled over spewing out vomit. Like a contagious disease. They retain their sights to the goal ahead and start moving towards the barbed wired boundary. It's tough going, every step is a lunge, deliberately forced to ensure not getting stuck. The wet weather had played its part on slowing down the section, leaving them in open ground for longer than they dare to want.

They were about ten feet from the wire when Taylor and Danns grabbed the dead soldiers body from the ground, tossing his body over the barbed wire for the men to use as a bridge, keeping clear from the razor like wire. Taylor was the last to get over. The men brake into a sprint to clear the gap between them and the trees. None looked back.

Chapter 6: The lone building

The trees were a welcome sight, the green of the grass and the smell of sweet wild flowers. The woodland teeming with life, rabbits, squirrels and the abundance of insects and spiders racing around. The apparent change of environment is overwhelming. The freshness in the atmosphere fills their nostrils, clean air passing through their lungs. The difference is like two planets in contrast. The dull grey stenched rotting trench life left behind.

They sit there catching their breath, each man unable to speak, the race towards the woodlands taking so much out of them. Ryan and Clarence recover quickly and head off on a recon. They steadily walk through to the edge of the wooded area, checking from side to side ensuring they were still alone, listening and watching for enemy. Reaching the other side of the forest they lay down in the tall grass, looking out over the valley.

150 meters away stands alone building, sitting tranquil in idyllic surrounding. "Could be housing an enemy machine gun nest" Rayan tells Clarence. They can see nothing stirring on the outside of the building, allowing any tell-tale signs of occupation. "We need to keep low" Ryan says, Clarence nods. The two lay there watching, waiting for any movement from the building.

Twenty minutes' pass and Sgt Taylor now recovered from his 1500-meter sprint sits up, "Come on lads let's go see what Ryan and Clarence are up to". The six of them get to their feet, each checking that nothing is left behind. Single file they walk towards the edge. They find Ryan and Clarence laying there watching the house, they join them adopting the prone position, staying low.

Sgt Taylor ask "Seen anything?" Ryan shakes his head in his reply "No… nothing … You want me to get closer?" Taylor nodding replies "Think you can?" Ryan without hesitation nods back "Sure no problem just keep a watch".
Ryan secures his personal webbing, checks his rifle. Places a round in the chamber. He begins to crawl, keeping low at all times, moving slowly but deliberate.

The situation now is too open for him, he's a sitting duck if there's a gun position here. His adrenalin pumping to near boiling point, his breathing erratic, uncontrollable, keeping his wits about him, he keeps going. Danns feels the danger in his bones, his experience tells him all is not right. "You should call him back Sarge… were out of range... Need to get closer if we're to give covering fire".

Sgt Taylor assessing the situation knowns the men can't go further without covering fire for them, as they too would be in the line of fire from any machine gun nest. "Can't do that… Too risky, if there's a gun nest there, we'll all be cut down… Shit should have waited till nightfall. "Taylor replies, anguish in his voice.

Fearful for his comrades' fate, Danns urges Taylor "Call him back Sarge! … He's a sitting duck out there; I don't like it… It's too quiet".

Ryan now half way towards the lone building. The others looking on. A flash of light from the right top window followed by the sound of machine gun fire. Sgt Taylor reacts first, cocking his Enfield rifle and taking aim releasing the round, identifying he's too far from the house to make an impact, they keep low scurrying closer to gain a better range.

It's too late, the sound of the guns echoed across the field. Dirt skirting in all directions, the impact on Ryan's body, jerking as he's hit numerous times is obvious, he stops moving, lying face down. The green of the grass now red.

Without warning Davies jumps to his feet in a flash, sheer anger flooding every part of his body, he charges towards the house yelling and screaming at the house, releasing around after round. Replacing magazine after magazine, bullets flying all directions.

Sgt Taylor yells, now standing. His voice is loud and desperate.
"Davies no… no stop... get back you don't stand a chance". His plea has fallen on deaf ears. The hail of bullets still showering down, Davies continuing his charge, reaches the house, out of breath he throws himself against the wall and releases the pin on the grenade, throwing it high and true. Hearing the sound of the grenade hitting the wooden floor. "Gnade...Gnade…" come the cries from the German machine gunners followed by the explosion. The machine gun is now silent.

Taylor and the rest of the section race towards the house. In the distance Davies collapses, hitting the ground hard. Danns, Clarence, Harold's and the two Nevells race through the house room by room clearing any dangers.

Sgt Taylor looks down to see Davies laying there. Multiple hits to his chest and legs, blood seeping from the wounds. Taylor kneels and cradles him like a child, he gives a brave smile. Davies waning pale body limp in his arms returns the smile.

"How did I do Sarge.... I got them… Yes?" his breathing shallow, choking on his own blood, Taylor looks at Davies, unable to give anything away on how Davies is, he speaks, his voice strong and commanding, "You did us proud… You're a real hero son... You got them all, your family would be proud …You probably saved our lives". Taylor holds him tighter, Davies eyes shed a tear, he knows his life is ending, he smiles one last time then draws his last breath, his head drops back and his body limp. Taylor can't hide the tears. He lays him down gently, removes Davies's tags. He reaches into Davies pocket and retrieves the letter Davies had promised to deliver. He places it into his tunic pocket, then stands. The men watch from the doorway, heads lowered and silent.

Danns is already half way across the field heading to where Ryan lays. He stoops over the body. Torn apart from the array of bullets ripping through him, leaving him unrecognised from his former self, Danns throws Ryan over his shoulder, turns and walks slowly back to the lone building. Harold's help him lay Ryan down as Danns removes Ryan's tags from his neck, places them in his pocket. Danns looks directly at Taylor, disgust showing. Danns livid at the loss of his companions, displays his grief, "You could have thought that out better!... didn't have to lose anyone today!" Now shouting, "**You were**

meant to get us all home" standing toe to toe with Taylor, grief taking over.

Sgt Taylor trying not to lose control, showing he is still in command of the section.
"I know". Guilt ridden unable to look him in the eye, with a sickening feeling in the bottom of his stomach he says "No more... let's get them buried".

The atmospheres darkened and the moral at an all-time low, anger seeping through their pores. All trust diminished.
Clarence and Young Neville start on the graves, whilst Danns makes two makeshift crosses, etching out the names of his fallen comrades. They stand, helmets in hands with their heads lowered as Taylor says a few words for his dead comrades.

Hours passed, yet no conversations exchanged. The silence adds to the macabre air as the mist of the night rises across the valley.

The dark skies of the night illuminated from the crescent moon, casting shadows over the valley. The tree line in the distance seeming denser more menacing, as if to invite some malevolent harm. Sergeant Taylor is perched by the upstairs window scanning the vast area for the

unwelcomed enemy. He breathes deeply, not his normal rhythm, feeling empty, saddened and lost.
The men losing respect, trust diminishing and the blame of the loss of their friends down to his leadership.

Sergeant Taylor is convinced more than ever he must now avoid any confrontation with the Germans and succeed in returning the rest back home.
Gazing out of the window, looking into the far and beyond the memories flood him like a swirling hurricane, his gaze so far, his watery eyes glazing his sight, he recalls the first day Davies joined his unit.

An ex officer demoted to the rank of rifleman. A man who was said to have disgraced his family name. The high ranking Davies family. It was back in July 1916 the battle of the Somme where some 58000 lives were lost, Captain Davies was given the task of ordering his company over the top. He had done this three times previously, sent out 250 men each time and only five or four came back, he wasn't able to send more men to certain death, after all nothing was gained. On his refusal, he was court martialled and branded a coward. He had hoped he had saved many lives that day for the sacrifice his own.

It was said the sergeant major carried out the duty that day, none returned, it had been the biggest loss in the Somme that day.

Captain Davies had been given the news in his cell. He tried to hang himself that night, the guard was alerted by the coughing and intervened. "If your gonna hang you coward …you will hang by the hand of the hang man … you bastard" cursed the guard spitting and kicking Davies.

The court martial had ordered Davies to be executed for cowardice. His uncle General Hubert Davies had asked for clemency and so he was speared only to join the front line as a rifleman. Taylor had taken a shine to Davies, he knew he was a decent man with high morals. Taylor also knew Davies didn't belong in this war, he was an intelligent man who would have been better equipped in civi street keeping the world ticking over.

The coffee smells good, it's broken his train of thought as the tin cup is handed to him. Danns looks straight at him. Both men now stood at the window.

"Sorry Sarge for earlier... Went off on one... Me and Ryan go way back... I know we never spoke about it... but we did

Sipping the hot coffee Sgt Taylor recognises the sorrow in Danns face, "So how you two meet… recruitment?"

"No… I remember him, his mum and his sister moving next door to us from Liverpool." replies Danns.
Sgt Taylor ask "which part of Yorkshire you from?
"Pudsey near Leeds" Danns replies, the thought of home makes him smile.
Sgt Taylor now settled and calm ask "you want to talk?"
Danns nods.

The two men sit on the wooden floor, sipping on the hot coffee. Danns offers his cigarettes to Taylor, both men draw on their cigarettes sending plumes of smoke high into the night sky.

Danns begins his story, images of a town with cobbled roads and the smell of fresh bread and kids playing in the streets flood his mind. "I remember the day he came up to me and offered me out; Just two scrawny kids trying to be cock of the street." gives out low laugh smiling broader now as the memories begin to flood around inside his head.

"I beat the shite out of him, however his mum kicked my arse; so my mum gave her some right verbal". looking at Taylor Danns continues his tale "When they first hit our street, they were spat at; His mum had lots of gentleman friends; You know the kind of girl she was, but you know how it was, it was how she made ends meet, they got by that way. She was a gorgeous redhead... always had money. More than us and our dad worked the pit."

"You two joined up the same time then" asked Sgt Taylor

Danns nods his head "Yeah the recruitment officer had our names down; The town folk all paraded the day we all marched out. Kate his sister gave me kiss and told me to make sure I got back home safe, said she had fancied me for years; Asked why I never asked her out."

"So didn't you ask her out" questions Taylor

"Me and Ryan were best mates and best mates don't mess with their sisters... not if you want to stay mates that is… she looks the double of her mother". Danns smiling, picturing the now young woman in his mind. Taylor sits upright "If she wants you… after the war, you gonna settle with her?"

Danns slips back into his depression, "How do I tell them Ryan is never coming back Sarge", a strong feeling of sadness creeps over him "how do you tell anyone?"

"I don't know… Guess you need to be made outta stone to do that", empathy creeping into Taylor's voice, knowing the heart ache of telling loved ones their kin folk have been killed, trying to put the right words together seems an impossible task to take on. "so how come you and Ryan never got on if you guys were best friends?" Taylor giving Danns a questioning look.

Danns looks deep, passed Taylor as if he weren't there. Taking him back to a time he wishes had never happened "we were taking out a group of German ambushers a year back ... We got them to surrender, Ryan had them covered, he wanted to take them prisoner, but me and the two lads we were with had a different view" his eyes closed tears rolled down his face, shaking his head, sighing heavily, choking on his words "we just shot them down ... they didn't have a chance ... Ryan never saw me in the same light since."
Taylor's face and voice displays compassion "We've all done something we're not proud off. But that won't change anything we done." They draw the last drag from the cigarettes and toss them into the empty fireplace. "Thanks Sarge ...Thanks for listening" Danns says, his emotions settling.

Harold climbs the wooden staircase, seeing the two men talking. He smiles an inward smile, knowing all will be ok tomorrow. Even with his withdrawn persona he reads the situation well, he takes in more than most credit him.

Harold's approaches the two men, "Sarge we've buried the three Germans at the back. Got this for you Danns, it's a Mauser C96 semi-automatic pistol, got a few 9mm clips too".

Danns reaches out and places it in the inside of his tunic. "Cheers Harold's, now tell the men to get their heads down" Danns replies grinning broadly, gratefully receiving the gift.

Sgt Taylor looks at Danns, a mocking tone in his voice. "You do know if you ever get caught by the Hun; They will bloody well execute you Danns".

Danns smiles, raises to his feet and walks to the far corner, "You know what Sarge …If I get caught then so be it" he smiles as he continues walking.

He lowers himself in the corner of the room, he finds his most comfortable position and gradually falls to sleep. Taylor looks on at the men sleeping, with tiredness creeping over him, his eyes close, he falls to sleep. A tormented sleep, images of death spiral inside his head, his body tossing and turning as the nightmares unfold. With Clarence's sleep disturbed. He keeps a watchful eye over him and the rest of the men.

Dawn breaks the darkness of the skies, the morning mist rising in the valley like a low fog. smoke escaping from the chimney pot meeting the clouds. The sun hiding, letting out streams of light.

Inside Clarence has the wood fire burning, the old iron pot resting on the hook. The smell of fresh coffee filling the room. Danns and the Neville's are enjoying a feast of the German rations of bratwurst in between doorstep cuts bread, while Harold's sits by the doorway puffing away on a twisted cigarette, choking as he inhales the smoke.

Sgt Taylor walks heavily down the wooden staircase almost tripping as he misses one step, still fatigued after his tormented sleep. The rest snigger as he almost falls. Taylor shrugs it off as if it never happened. Clarence passes Taylor a mug of the fresh coffee, he accepts it gratefully, sipping delicately as not to burn his lips. In silence the soldiers tidy themselves and recheck their weapons.

As time passes the restlessness sets in. They pack their personal belonging into their packs. Sgt Taylor addresses the men. "I understand the feelings you guys have and I agree, we should have waited till nightfall before coming here; Believe me I am truly sorry and I wish I could turn back time... but I can't."

The men nod, Conor Neville walks towards Taylor, with a friendly face he speaks to Taylor. "It was gonna happen sooner or later Sarge ... just hard for all of us... but I still trust you... I know words were said in haste last night, but we need you too."

Sgt Taylor places his right hand on Conor's shoulder addressing the group. "Thanks lad... OK... let's get moving."
The section heads off through the doorway, walking into a beautiful summer's day as the sun now beating down over the valley, the now warm peaceful and calm day. Ryan and Davies, nothing more than a memory.

Chapter 7: You need to decide

Two days had passed since leaving the lone building and they hadn't seen anyone, not a native, not a soul. It was as if they were the only survivors of this dreadful bloody war. Marching through the country side, the green of the meadows with the clean flowing fresh water streams, they take time watching the wild life, taking in the surroundings. It's as if they had never seen it all before, the tranquil sound of the countryside allowing them to relax, feeling more at ease.

They settle at the edge of the dense forest, overlooking the fields spreading far beyond their vision. Feeling good that they may now at last make it home, without any confrontations with the enemy. Spirits were heightened.

Happy to relax the survivors bed for the night after another day's march. Andy Neville is place on first watch. He beds himself into the shrubbery, camming up so to blend with his surroundings while the others sleep.

The smell of cordite awakens them from their slumber, the crack of rifle fire in the distance. Andy Neville breaks from the cover of the wooded crop keeping low, eyes squinted, almost trying to make out the silhouettes in the night light. Flashes and the rifle shots in distance more frequent and the harrowing sound of wars casualties creeping ever closer.

Now the section had been disturbed, dread flowing through them like a freight train, fear filling their senses. All their rifles posed and ready for a fight. The sickening feeling that all is lost churning in their stomachs. Andy Neville looking towards the silhouettes whispering "Is that friend or foe"

Danns quickly answers the question "That's foe Andy... listen there talking kraut"

Sgt Taylor realises that they must move now, if they are to be safe. He knows they will be more casualties; this does not bode well with him. Scanning the battle field, he turns his attention to address his men.

"We need to get passed them; Must be no more than 500 feet away. Need to keep quiet! We'll take the tree line left as far as we can... need to get around these bastards without been seen"

Danns realising the enemy have closed in and they must have passed them at some stage to be set up in trenches this far up, The French hold out must have crumbled, without meaning to he voices his opinion to the rest of them. "The Huns are further into France than we thought; Our best chances are probably trying to get to friendly units; The sea is 100's of mile off yet, and the chance of not running into the enemy are slim"

Sgt Taylor nods in agreement "You could be right Danns, but before we do... think about it ... you lot need to decide... Do we carry on for the sea or try for friendly units?". They glance over each other, each seeking some kind of approval from the next.

They were still thinking on what action to take, when Clarence speaks first. "I think we should see how far we get... Who knows we may just make it out of here".

Danns still thinking he's on borrowed time looks directly at Clarence, his finger pointing down towards the German trench. "We have come a long way I know... and to some of you... Well could be right to carry on with this desertion lark, but you know ... I think we need to face our demons head on"
They look at Danns quizzical and wondering what's brought this on. Only three weeks earlier he was along with Taylor encouraging them to desert, as this was most likely the only way they would ever see home again. Confused they look to Taylor for the answer.

Through all this time the battle continued as the sound of rifle and mortar fire echoe in the cold shadow of night.

Taylor quietly whispers "Look men... We need to decide and quickly," without hesitation Harold's agrees with Danns along with the Neville brothers. Clarence nods his head too, a smile breaking out at the corner of his mouth.

Taylor gives the orders "Check you rifles... load up, fix bayonets". The men cock their weapons and attach the bayonets ready to engage the enemy. The six men knowing what's expected of them, non-wanting to let the other down. Keeping low to the ground, under the cover of night they move closer to the enemy, the sound of the battle growing louder with every move.

The allied lines hit hard as the German bombardment continues, exploding debris flying all directions, cutting the allied soldiers down with the razor like fragments. The sound of the mortar commanders yelling orders in the German lines for continuous fire. Never letting up. The harrowing screams from the casualties haunting Taylor, the others tormented from the sounds.

Taylor decides they have to take out a few of the mortar crews to give the allies a fighting chance.

Clarence volunteers saying he will head in first with the grenades, followed by 2 or 3 with guns blazing. Taylor informs them, he and Danns will go tail end Charlie mopping up as they go.

The men know this could be their last battle and not what they all agreed to three weeks ago. They shake hands and wish each other luck and hope luck will be on their side and get them through this.

Clarence stands ready followed by the rest, he checks his pockets are full with grenades, six in all, he turns to Taylor, and smiles "Meet you on the other side boss" with that he dashes down the valley wall towards the German lines, not giving anyone chance to reply. His long legs now in full stride almost on top of the enemy, he unpins two grenades and tosses them at either side as he leaps over the trench. His body collapsing with a roll and back to his feet as he hits the ground, unclipping two more and offering them at the two mortar nest.

The first set explode, followed quickly by a second explosion. Devastation hits the mortar nest, flinging the enemy high into the air, ripping the bodies apart. The Neville's follow, jumping into the trench, round after round like two crazies, inflicting death on whoever crossed their path, no mercy given. The Germans are caught off guard. Harold hits the trench some ten foot further down, releasing shot after shot, clip after clip, the quiet shy young man turned demonised, punishing the enemy. Danns and Taylor come in mopping up the last are that still standing. The six men have destroyed sixty lives in less than five minutes.

All six men now stand on the forward edge of the trench facing in, breathing short rapid breaths, their adrenalin pumping, they continue to shoot down any German soldier who dares to retaliate and show courage under fire.

Taylor yells frantically "Get your arses outa here... fucking move now"

The trench is re-enforced, some thirty or so Germans shooting as they start to appear. The men turn giving no thought of who's now behind them. legs tiring as they start to sprint into nomans land. The six men, scattered formation breathing sharp, unable to take in air, just running as fast as their legs will allow.

The German Oberschutze now above the trench adopt the kneeling position and take aim. The crack of rifle fire echoes in the valley, Harold's buckles. Almost somersaulting over as he is hit three times in the back, Taylor tries to reach him but Danns pulls him away,

"Sarge it's too late for him run... just ... run". They continue to run, Taylor checking to see if Harold's moving, he's not.

The soldiers in the allied trench are cheering, willing them on. It's a mix of British and French together. The chants continue louder and louder.
The trench falls silent as another volley of shots echoes through nomans land; this time the men are lucky.

Clarence stops running, looks over at the other four. He knows if he can destroy the German snipers the rest could make it.
The Neville's pass him wondering why he's stopped "Go on lads get going" says Clarence urging them on. Danns and Taylor haven't noticed this as there further down the line.

Clarence looks down at his chest, blood is evident on his tunic, seems he too was hit by the first volley. He opens his tunic to find the exit hole in his chest

Feeling the bubbling in his chest and throat he runs towards the Germans picking up speed as he sprints forward, he unclips the last two grenades, still going forward. Another volley aimed at Clarence sounds. He drops to his knees allowing the grenades to fall rolling German bound. The sound of the explosion confirms his target. The rifle fire has ceased, as the enemy lay scattered in the dirt.

Clarence takes his last look over his shoulder, he smiles as he watches, the corners of his mouth turn up as sees the others cross into the allied trench. Clarence lays down slowly onto his back, looking skyward, the brightness of a thousand stars looking down upon him from a heavenly sky. "Well God …Looks like you win …not like I have somewhere else to go …I hope you're ready because I on my way" Clarence says through his laboured breaths. He has the best view in the house. How beautiful it seems. He rolls his head to face the trench, knowing he's given his all, he closes his eyes for the final time. Darkness falls upon him.

The four survivors are given a hero's welcome. The alcohol flowing, French and British troops eagerly wanting to shake their hands recognising their bravery.

The French and British infantry officers offer their hands to Taylor, thanking him and his men for silencing the mortars. Taylor explains it was no more than two or three, however on his reckoning he and his men had taken out sixty to eighty soldiers. Taylor reaches for the small ammo box out of his satchel and hands it to the British officer. "We collected these so their loved ones would know they have fallen" Taylor says as the officer shakes his hand one more time. His face kind and thoughtful "thank-you
sergeant... please thank your men for their part in this too." He steps back and salutes the four survivors.

Danns and the two Neville's are sat at a table drinking rum in the dugout accommodation, listening to the stories been told, their glass never emptying, the allied soldiers constantly refilling them. Tonight they are heroes.

Chapter 8: A final farewell

08:30 am 19th November 1918

One year later in Southampton. Just eight days after the Prime minister announced the armistice was signed by Marshal Ferdinand Foch's, Matthias Erzberger and Admiral Rosslyn Wemyss at 05:00 hours on the 11th November 1918. The docks are lined with the wives, girlfriends, mums, dads and their children waiting for the survivors and the ships to return. The sound of jubilation roars across the piers as the brass bands march to the sound of their compositions as the ship's enter into port. The Battle worn soldiers begin to disembark.

Families embrace each other so close, happy tears falling, laughing and shouting, for many the occasion is too much. Both the returning men and waiting families, break down through sheer exhaustion and excitement. The pier is packed, no room to maneuver, the families reuniting by the thousands.

The 2nd lieutenant walks down the gantry towards the solid ground of the docks. His feet touch for the first time in four years, the country where he was born. The feeling of jubilation overloads his body, the shivers running through him so hard to describe. Him being one out of the

many men who had fought. He had survived to the end.
The war was finally over.

Soldiers passed him on the foot of the gantry, he offers
his hand and wishes them well, they salute him in return,
before continuing to their awaiting loved ones.
The Sergeant halts, his head turns towards the officer, a
smile runs the length of his face, it was the familiar face
of someone he once knew who stood there.
"Lieutenant...well how the bloody hell did you ever make
that rank" The officer exchanges the smile and offers his
hand, they shake a hardy handshake, this turning into an
embrace. Almost teary the two men exchange words.
"And how the hell did you make the rank of sergeant"
replies the officer. The sergeant retreats one step,

"Good to see you Danns ...or should I say sir?" Danns ask
the sergeant if he would like to join him for a brew,
pointing at the small tea shop further the road. The
sergeant accepts enthusiastically as the two men walk
side by side down the pier and head for the small tea shop
on the harbour promenade, they open the door to find a
packed room full of service men and women   sat on the
small wooden chairs surrounding the tatty wooden square
tables.

They notice a table for two available deep into the room next to the counter. No sooner they sit down, a young teenage girl rushes towards them, her shoulder length auburn hair tied back, her white pinafore stained from tea and cakes, more grey than white. Her freckled face smiling, her hazel eyes focusing on Danns uniform. "What can I get you gentlemen" she asks, Danns orders two teas and two slices of their freshly baked trench cake. With that the young girl retreats to the counter.

Danns looks across the table, the sergeant looks tired, worn out probably from the travelling. "You ok Conor …You look tired" Asked Danns, Conor half smiles "Just been hectic these last few days with the evacuation out of France …Placed me in charge of the wounded and the return of the injured prisoners."

The girl returns with their order and places the tray on the table interrupting Conors tale, Danns reaches into his trench coat pocket and takes out his wallet, giving the girl two shiny shilling pieces. Her eyes wide and brightened, she stares at the coins, "sorry sir this is too much money" she says in her apologetic tone. Conor brushes her away with a wave of his arm saying "keep the change dear". The Young girl walks away looking offended as if she had just been scolded.

The two men sip from the cups then engage in conversation. "So Conor how come you made sergeant … You were only a private when you left for your new unit". Conor sits back on his chair, takes another drink from his cup then unfolds his story.

"It goes back to the day after we stormed the German trench, you remember, you and Taylor had gone to the 3rd brigade while me and Andy were left behind. Their commander thought we had done a brave job in silencing the mortars he promoted us both to lance corporal, then that started the ball rolling, I got a detail to collect some intel from the German trench, I managed to get the information and we got the engineers to dig under our trench to theirs, then blew it up from underneath them, that earned me my second stripe"

Danns takes in a deep breath, removes the cigarette from the package and lights it, Conor refuses the offer of a cigarette and continues his tale.

"This is when the push back started, we had cleared the destroyed trench and moved further into France gaining ground towards the German boarders, over the next six to seven weeks we marched forward gaining ground every day.

On one such occasion we came under heavy enemy fire during an assault to clear a forest." The sergeant gives a heavy sigh, Danns opposite sits there, his concentration fixed on Conor's every word.

"We lost a lot of men that day, I was lucky ...You could say God had a hand in it, a tree fell just inches away from me, knocking me off my feet ...That's when the gun fire started, killing most of the troop, our second line came up after us wiping out their gun post and cleared the enemy line, I went in like a mad man having just witnessed my section mowed down. Pretty much how I got my third stripe what about you? How did you become an officer?" Pointing at the pip on Danns shoulder.

Danns gives off a shallow laugh, "Pretty much the same as you, I had many small confrontations with the Germans, many costing dearly on both sides," His memory takes him back, searching his past. "Taylor and I went out many times, he got me my third stripe after I carried him back form one particular encounter, when he got shrapnel in his back from a building we blew up and then a few weeks later we went out on a major sortie, we got most of the way pushing hard against the German trench lines when we suffered a counter attack, half of the battalion had fallen, Taylor got forty men to help him with the evac of the wounded while I took command and cleared the German trench, like you this was the start of a new offensive gaining essential ground towards the surrender of the Germans."

He takes a pause, placing the stub of the cigarette into the ash tray and downing the rest of his tea. Wiping his mouth with the back of his right hand he continues, "I got back to camp victorious and with the relevant information on the German campaign.

We had also taken many prisoners that day. Taylor was stood there looking smug with our Colonel by his side, it was then I became an officer …I tried to refuse it but was told to man up, I was then put in charge of my own troop of sixty men, Taylor was told he was to be my troop sergeant, so I got my own back on him, got to say we became good friends" with that said Danns face turns, no longer a smile but stern, he drifts off into another world, his mind going to places and a time he would prefer to leave far behind him. Back to a time of smog and the smell of death and cordite, back sat in the dull grey clay coloured trench.

"Any news on Taylor. Did he make it? "asked the Sergeant, Danns looks into the distance... a memory flooding back. He pictures the scene as clearly as if he was back there.

"Sadly not... We were told the war had finished ...Me and Taylor had stayed together throughout. We had some seventy prisoners and decided to allow the German prisoners to be released; Myself, been the lowest ranked officer was given the task, Sergeant Taylor and two others helped me lead the party into no man's land and to meet with their Officers. We did the normal handshake and exchange of peacekeeping gifts"

Danns pauses as the memory fills his thoughts and a shudder rolls down his spine, the felling of grief shadowing the reunion of the two men. "We heard the crack of a rifle firing, the bullet went straight through Taylor's neck, almost ripped his head off! He didn't stand a chance, he died instantly... I don't think he even knew". Genuine sadness travelled through his words. "He had survived all that time from the very beginnings... even survived the Somme; To suffer at the hands one man looking for his next notch on his rifle butt; Didn't work out that well for him too.

The German officer executed the bastard in front of our lines ...Was to send a message that no more killing was to take place."

The sergeant lowers his head in sorrow for the loss of a brave man he once fought with. A man he held in high regard. "He was a great man; I will always remember him. He didn't deserve to die like that". Conor's heart sank, his stomach tied up in knots, pain from the knowledge his old comrade had fallen.

Danns places his hand on his friend's hands tightly to comfort him. "And Andy, where's Andy?"

Sergeant Neville looks at Danns, a smile appears and his eyes brighten. "The lucky little bastard got out of the war early... took a bullet in the leg and shoulder... (gives a little chuckle) was hit and miss at first... you know what those field hospitals were like"

"So he survived?" replied Danns a big wide smirk on his face.
"Yes his arm works well, a bit stiff this time of year, lost the lower part of his left leg; But that doesn't stop him, old peg leg now. Helps mum with the farm... that's where I'm going now. You know Danns if ever you need somewhere to go, you're always welcome after all I owe you for saving my life".

The men shake hands for the last time. They never did meet again.

Chapter Nine: The Letter

The cold of the December winds swirling the lose snow high, the snowflakes drifting covering all. The rooftops covered in white, the glassy tapered icy stalagmite draping from the gutters, droplets of water hitting the soft snowed covered paths. A warm glow from the high sun evading the cotton wool clouds, sending a false signal for the day, it looks warm, but the temperatures are hitting the lows. Windows iced over, the many patterns etched in the ice. All now at peace now the war is over.

The small garden surrounding the little town house is covered in snow, a boy and his mother are playing. The snowman is almost complete; laughing at the carrot on the face of the snowman, a bendy red carrot hanging off the face, looking like he had been in a boxing match. They stop instantly, a tall stranger is stood at their gate. A tall uniformed man.

The heavy wooden door to house opens, an elderly woman appears, she stands watching the stranger, her demeanor is straight and strong as if to be protecting her young, her tone is somberly "Hello stranger how can we help you… are you lost"

The tall stranger stands at the gate and faces the elderly woman "I'm looking for Lucy and a boy Robert" he replies.

The young women holds her child close and stands rigid to the spot, her eyes transfixed on the stranger. Who was he? what does he want from them? Lucy's could feel herself getting warmer, her face now flushed, she didn't like a stranger knowing her boys name let alone hers.

The stranger introduces himself, his voice strong and clear, "Please accept my apologies and forgetting my manners …My name is Danns… 2nd lieutenant Danns… I served in the 1st battalion rifles division in France and I had a friend who wanted to give you some letters we found on your husband. He couldn't make it so here I am".

Danns has the letters in his hand, outstretched arm offering them. Not as confident now and not too sure if he should be there at all, he takes a steps back away from the gate.

The young woman moves passed her son urging him to stay, she slowly walks towards Danns, choking back on her words with sorrowfulness. "I'm Lucy... we had notification over a year ago informing us my husband had been killed" feeling uneasy she continues to go forward towards the gate, looking back at her son. He appears scared, but stands where he was left, he doesn't move just keeps his eyes on his mother.

"I understand" says Danns, feeling uncomfortable, maybe even naïve to think he could just walk in, his nervousness showing. "I need to give you these as... I promised two of the bravest men I had known... And if I survived, I swore I would get them to you" Images of Taylor and Davies fill his mind, the sick feeling of loss churns in his stomach. Danns head drops to his chest, "I'm truly sorry for your loss", He turns and starts to retreat back up the steep snow covered road, Danns walks slowly but deliberately, not looking back.

Lucy watches the stranger leave, heading back up the hill. She realises Danns is fulfilling a promise, a promise he had made to his two fallen friends. Her heart skips as she remembers her Stanley, her mind's eye pictures him, stood next to her saying I do, dressed in his cotton suit, his curly hair flattened and greased back, the priest looking on. Lucy smiles an inner smile as the image changes to the day she told him she had become pregnant, his kind eyes staring back, tears start to form uncontainable, rolling down her face, her image slowly disappears, Stanley vanishes, diminishing into a shapeless shape to nothingness.

She opens the gate wiping away the tears and races towards Danns "Please stop please".

Danns turns his head to discover Lucy racing up the street towards him, she stops, freezes on the spot, her chest heaving rapidly as the cold fills her lungs. Lucy's eyes widen as Danns turns and walks towards her, fear and excitement fusing through her body. The letters now in Lucy's hand. Snow settling on them as they momentarily stand silently face to face.

She smiles, a warm kind radiant smile, Lucy links her left arm around his right arm. Looking up to his face she ask, "Please join us for some tea". Arms linked they step into the garden. The little boy, his mum and the stranger enter the house. The door closes.

The End.